D0396502

A boatload of Roses

The English Roses

Catch the Bouquet!

CALLAWAY ARTS & ENTERTAINMENT

19 FULTON STREET, FIFTH FLOOR, NEW YORK, NEW YORK 10038

PUFFIN BOOKS

Published by the Penguin Group
Penguin Young Readers Group, 345 Hudson Street, New York, New York 10014, U.S.A.
Penguin Group (Canada), 90 Eglinton Avenue East, Suite 700, Toronto, Ontario,
Canada M4P2Y3 (a division of Pearson Penguin Canada Inc.)

Penguin Books Ltd., Registered Offices: 80 Strand, London WC2R 0RL, England

First published in the United States of America by Callaway Arts & Entertainment and Puffin Books, 2010

1 3 5 7 9 10 8 6 4 2

First Edition

Produced by Callaway Arts & Entertainment
Nicholas Callaway, President and Publisher
John Lee, CEO
Cathy Ferrara, Managing Editor and Production Director
Toshiya Masuda, Art Director
Nelson Gómez, Director of Digital Technology
Amy Cloud, Senior Editor
Bomina Kim, Design Assistant
Ivan Wong, Jr. and José Rodríguez, Production
Jennifer Caffrey, Executive Assistant

Special thanks to Doug Whiteman and Mariann Donato.

Library of Congress Cataloging-in-Publication Data is available.

Puffin Books ISBN 978-0-14-241129-2

Printed in the United States of America

www.madonna.com www.callaway.com www.penguin.com/youngreaders

All of Madonna's proceeds from this book will be donated to Raising Malawi (www.raisingmalawi.org), an orphan-care initiative.

The English Roses
by MADONNA
With Amy Cloud
Catch the Bouquet!
PUFFIN
CALLAWAY
New York
2010
illustrated by
jeffrey fulvimari
Book 12

Contents
Hello, hello???

CHAPTER I

A Message from Your

NEW MESSAGE
To: Dear Readers
From: Your Very Important Narrator
Subject: ENGLISH ROSES, DUH!

Dearest Reader,

So, word has gotten around that you have never heard of the English Roses. (Don't worry about who told me; it's classified information!) I feel that as a V.I.N. (that's Very Important Narrator to you), it is my duty to let you in on the

only news that's worth knowing: the English Roses are five funky, fresh, fashionable friends; and their names are as follows: Binah Rossi, Nicole Rissman, Grace Harrison, Amy Brook, and Charlotte Ginsberg. These glam girls spend almost all of their time together doing what most twelve-year-old females tend to do: shopping, cooking, IM-ing, consuming vast amounts of sugar, giggling till their sides ache, cute-boy watching. . . . This list could go on forever! Though each is as different and unique as, well, a snowflake, the fivesome really is the best of friends, and they help one another through everything—good times and bad, excitement and boredom, bad-hair days, red-letter days, and everything in between. Because, dear reader, that's just what best friends do! Period.

As sixth graders at Hampstead School in London, England, the English Roses had quite a fabulous year. But all fabulous things must come to an end, and that year was over. With seventh grade—and junior high—looming ahead, the English Roses were trying to squeeze the most out of the last lazy bits of summer. There were only four weeks left, and though that can seem like an ice age to a small child, to the Roses it was going by in a flash! A summer filled with ice cream, picnics, lazy Saturdays, boat rides, beach trips, and shopping will tend to do that, you know.

Like all wonderful summers, this one contained a bit of romance. Well, actually, quite a lot of romance. And a wedding. And five tap dancing elves with twenty fingers and four eyes each. (Just kidding! I had to make sure you were paying attention, you see?)

So what happened, you ask? What's the deal? Well, you'll simply have to wait until the next chapter to find out. And anyway, the only point of my message was to let you in on who the English Roses are. So, please excuse me. Now that I've done my work here, I have other very important business to attend to.

With fondest wishes,

Your Very Important Narrator

CHAPTER 2

A Shepherd's Pie to Remember

"Ernesta, you are the best-a, I must confess-a . . ." Binah Rossi softly sang as her pet gerbil, Ernesta, pounced happily in her cage nearby. Even though her sensible and book-savvy best friend, Nicole, always claimed that the furry animal couldn't understand

Binah's songs ("Her brain is the size of a pea, after all," Nicole would say as if reciting from a science textbook), Binah was somehow certain that Ernesta enjoyed the little tunes she sang, especially when she was cooking.

Binah simply adored singing. Her mother had loved to sing while she cooked, too, or so Binah's papa told her. It made Binah happy to think that she and her mother shared this small joy; it was as if she had inherited something special from her. Since her mum had died when she was just a baby, Binah didn't remember much about her, but she still missed her. Funny how you can miss someone you didn't even really know to begin with, isn't it?

Binah was busy in the kitchen making her father's favorite dinner: shepherd's pie. But this

wasn't your average shepherd's pie, oh no! (Side note: in case you didn't know, shepherd's pie is a meat pie with a mashed-potato topping. Are your mouths watering yet? Well, please don't drool on me! Thank you.) She liked to make this signature British dish her own by crumbling bits of crackers in with the potatoes on top and adding ginger and shredded cheese to the mixture of meat inside.

Papa loved Binah's shepherd's pie more than anything else she cooked for him. (Since there were just the two of them, Binah cooked a lot.

And cleaned a lot. And did the laundry a lot. And did pretty much everything else that needs to be done when a mother is not around a lot. Luckily, her four besties helped her with her chores a lot.) And today her father had requested it specially. As he and Binah were having breakfast that morning, he had mentioned that Miss Fluffernutter was coming to dinner and how much he would love if she would make her shepherd's pie for them.

"Miss Fluffernutter and I have something we want to tell you," her papa had said, his eyes bright and shining.

It warmed Binah's heart to see her father so happy. Since he and Miss Fluffernutter had begun spending so much time together earlier in the school year, she saw his smile more frequently than she could ever remember.

Oh, please! Don't tell me you don't know Miss Fluffernutter! She's only the English Roses' number one most favorite teacher in the whole wide world. She taught them way back in fifth grade but remained a benevolent presence in their lives through sixth grade. In a nutshell, Miss Fluffernutter is a frizzy-haired, funny, and friendly teacher with a heart of gold. She's the kind of person who always seems to know what's bothering you and, more importantly, always seems to know how to help.

Anyway, as I was saying, Binah's father and Miss Fluffernutter had been spending a lot of time together over the past six months. Coffee dates, dinner dates, movie dates, museum dates—you name it! I should also mention that the two love-birds almost always included Binah on their dates. To some of you that may seem strange—the idea of two lovey-dovey grown-ups wanting a twelve-year-old along on their romantic rendezvous—but Miss F. loved spending time with Binah as much as Binah loved spending time with her. Miss F. always had fun, interesting activities in mind for them to do—things like visiting water parks, horseback riding, and even playing paint ball!

Binah was most pleased that her father was spending time with someone who made him happy, especially someone as lovely and wonderful as Miss Fluffernutter. She really couldn't ask for a better person for her father to date. And seeing that sad, empty look on her father's face replaced with a smile made her heart soar with joy.

Binah opened the oven and slid the shepherd's pie inside. Done! Now she could get back to her newest hobby, knitting. She plopped down in a

kitchen chair and picked up her needles and yarn. Binah found something very comforting about knitting: the repetitive *click-click* of the needles clacking against each other, the satisfaction of creating something from nothing. It was yet another activity she was prompted to learn after hearing that her mother had loved to knit. Binah liked to sit in a reverie and think about what it would have

been like if she and her mother could have spent time knitting together, or daydream about her number one all-time major crush, Ben.

Just then the door to their old townhouse creaked open. "Hello, hello?" Mr. Rossi called. He was followed by a bouncy Miss Fluffernutter, whose hair, Binah thought, seemed even fluffier than usual. It created a frizzy halo around her rosy cheeks and sparkling blue eyes. She was wearing a colorful patchwork sundress and brown sandals that clasped around her ankles and a big, bright smile. A strand of wooden beads hung around her neck, and her nails were painted quite a stunning shade of purple.

"Well, hello, dear! You look lovely, as always! Give me a big hug. Oh, what are you knitting there? Is it a hat? I hope so! I simply love hand-knit hats. Something so cozy about them, you know! Not that we need coziness in the summer, mind you. But coziness is always a bit nice, don't you

think? Mmmm, something smells simply delightful!" As usual, words tumbled out of Miss Fluffernutter's mouth at a frenetic speed. Binah felt a bit dizzy simply listening to her.

The three sat down to dinner, and after the last savory bits had been scraped from their plates, just as Binah was going to start clearing away the dishes, her father cleared his throat.

"Binah, Miss Fluffernutter and I have an . . . announcement," he said, his voice sounding a bit shaky. He glanced nervously at Miss Fluffernutter, who smiled confidently and squeezed his hand.

"What is it, Papa?" Binah asked, curious.

"Well," her father began, "as you know, the two of us have grown . . . fond of each other over the past six months."

"Yes," Miss Fluffernutter beamed. "Quite fond!"

"You see," Mr. Rossi continued, "I've asked Miss Fluffernutter to marry me. And she accepted!"

Miss Fluffernutter turned to Binah. "But we wanted to see how you felt about it, Binah."

Binah was so surprised that her last bite of food almost fell from her mouth right into her glass of milk! She tried to speak, but every thought seemed to have vanished from her head.

"I-I'm," she stuttered, searching for the right words. Quickly, she recovered. "I'm really happy for you both," she said.

"We both realize this is a sudden announcement, and I'm sorry I didn't come to you first, but we were so excited that we couldn't wait," Binah's father explained.

"When will the wedding be?" Binah asked.

"Well, that's the thing," Miss Fluffernutter began. "We were hoping to do it before school starts."

Binah, ever polite, couldn't help but blurt, "But that's only a month away!"

"That's true," her father began, "but we aren't having anything big or fancy. Just a simple ceremony will do—something outside, maybe."

"I just love the idea of an outdoor wedding," Miss Fluffernutter gushed. She paused. "Binah," she continued. "We both understand that this is a lot to take in. Please let us know how you're feeling."

Binah didn't know what to say. She was still shocked from the news; she couldn't even begin to process how she felt about it. On the one hand, she was overjoyed that her papa and Miss Fluffernutter were so happy. And she simply adored Miss Fluffernutter; what better stepmum could she ask for? On the other hand, something about the news felt strange. And she couldn't exactly tell what that something was.

She raised her milk glass. "Cheers!" she said, smiling. "I'm so glad for both of you."

Except that deep down inside she wasn't.

???
...cheers...

CHAPTER 3

Dress Distress

Three days later, Binah and the rest of the English Roses were in Marks & Spencer department store, searching for a dress for Binah to wear to the wedding. Miss Fluffernutter had asked Binah to be her bridesmaid, which meant that she would have to walk down the aisle ahead of Miss F. and stand nearby while Miss F. and Papa exchanged their wedding vows.

"Wedding vows." The words still sounded rather funny to her. She couldn't believe that her papa was actually getting married!

Anyway, usually the bride picks out the dress she wants her bridesmaids to wear, but Miss Fluffernutter told Binah she could wear whatever she wanted as long as it was blue. So Binah did what any twelve-year-old in her position would do:

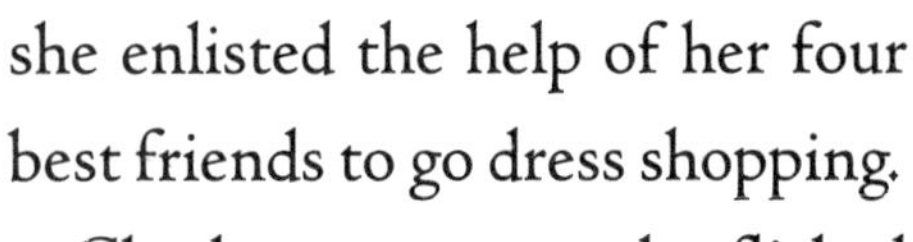

she enlisted the help of her four best friends to go dress shopping.

Charlotte, ever posh, flicked her shiny black hair behind her shoulder and fingered her pearl (real, natch) earrings. In her arms she clutched several binders, each dedicated to a different aspect of wedding planning and preparation. Upon hearing the news of the upcoming nuptuals, Charlotte had appointed herself "official" wedding planner and immediately bought a stack of magazines from which to glean inspiration on dresses, flowers, centerpieces, and a variety of other items. Charlotte had been planning her own wedding (in her mind, that is) since the tender age

of six, so the chance to help plan someone else's seemed like a dream come true.

Charlotte had also kindly volunteered her family's spacious gardens for the wedding (the Ginsberg family was—how shall I put this?—mad rich. They lived in a mansion and had a butler, a cook, and even a driver!).

Amy emerged from the dressing room. "Isn't this dress totally divine?" she cooed, prancing

around like a fashion model in a strapless silk number. Amy was obsessed with clothes and style; she had even modeled in Teen Fashion Week the previous spring.

Nicole, ever the sensible one, eyed the price tag. "With a divine price to go along with it," she said.

Grace heaved a sigh, clearly wishing she was kicking around a football (that's a soccer ball to you Americans) instead of shuffling about a clothing store. "Have you found anything yet, Binah?" she asked. "No offense, but I'm missing a game on TV."

"These dresses seem really expensive," Binah said worriedly, fingering the price tag of a floral frock. "Papa said to buy whatever I want, but I feel guilty spending this much on me when the wedding is already costing loads of money."

Charlotte's voice could be heard from deep within a rack of gowns. "You shouldn't worry about the price, Binah," she advised. "This is a once-in-a-lifetime event, and you should look absolutely gorg. I mean, how often does your father get married?" She emerged from the rack with two more dresses,

The happy couple shops for a wedding cake.

which she held next to Binah. "And especially to a supercool woman like Miss Fluffernutter!"

"I'm totally jealous, Binah." Amy sighed, twirling in front of a full-length mirror. "I mean, Miss Fluffernutter is so amazing as a teacher. Imagine how she'll be as a stepmum!"

"Yeah," Grace said. "You're so lucky, Binah."

"I know." Binah paused shyly. "Did I tell you guys where she took me last week?"

Amy frowned. "The art museum?"

Binah shook her head. "No, that was two weeks ago."

"The beach?" Grace suggested.

"Nope," Binah replied. "Actually, this was better, because it ended up solving a little, um, problem I was having." She looked at her friends expectantly.

"Ohhhhhh!!" they said in unison, nodding their heads. The English Roses knew all too well about Binah's infamous "problem."

Here is the deal: you know how when a girl starts . . . growing up . . . she needs certain "garments" to help her out? Certain undergarments? Certain undergarments that start with a "b" and end with an "a"? I think we both know what I'm getting at here. You see, the female students at Hampstead School had begun wearing bras at the beginning of fifth grade. Some had even started in the fourth grade. But now the girls were leaving sixth grade, and still Binah was the only girl she knew who went bra-less.

And what was the reason, you may ask, for her lack of full frontal support? Well, as you may recall (and certainly should know by now), Binah grew up without a mother. For her entire life, it has been just she and her father weathering life's storms. But a girl can't just go to her father with such a personal, "womanly" matter. Or, at least, Binah didn't feel comfortable doing so. Of course, her dear friends offered up their own mums to go bra shopping with Binah, but she didn't feel right about that, either.

So she was relieved when Miss Fluffernutter suggested they go shopping without her father the previous week. "A little shopping trip, just us girls," she had said.

"So we went to Harrods," Binah explained to her friends, "and Miss Fluffernutter and the salesgirl helped me find three bras!" She grinned happily. "I don't have to worry about it this year!"

"That's awesome, Binah!" her friends chorused. They were overjoyed that their best friend finally had a mother figure in her life. None of the other Roses could quite imagine life without her own mum.

"Miss Fluffernutter is going to be the best mum ever!" Charlotte told Binah as she gave her a hug.

Binah smiled as she hugged her friend back.

But in her deepest of hearts, something about Charlotte's statement bothered her. "But I already have a mum," she wanted to say. "She's watching over me from heaven."

She wondered if her mum was watching her now.

CHAPTER 4

Boxes in the Parlor

Binah hummed a happy tune as she opened her front door. She placed her keys on the hallway table as usual, and went to visit Ernesta. The tiny creature was happily running on her exercise wheel. Binah scooped up Ernesta and nuzzled her cheek against the animal's soft fur.

She went into her bedroom and placed a gigantic garment bag in her closet among the simple skirts, vests, blouses, and other "boring" clothes that made up her wardrobe. Binah wasn't much for fashion, but even she had to admit that inside the bag was the most beautiful dress she had ever seen. Charlotte and the other Roses had convinced her

to buy it for the wedding; it was more expensive than the dresses Binah usually bought for fancy occasions (which were few and far between, as Binah and her father really didn't have much money), but Amy had used her mother's connections to get the dress at a great discount. (Amy's mum worked as a buyer at Marks & Spencer. I know, I know, don't we all wish our mums had such cool jobs? Le sigh!)

Binah had felt like an absolute princess when she tried on the dress. It was a royal blue silk that seemed to perfectly match the color of her eyes, and it was strapless! (Can you believe it? She wasn't even sure her papa would allow her to wear it!) It fit her like a glove; even the stylish saleswoman had commented on how stunning Binah looked.

PRINCESS BINAH!!!
Ta-
-da

Binah had never been *to* a wedding before, much less *in* one, so she hadn't been aware that bridesmaids got to wear such beautiful garments! Maybe this bridesmaid thing wouldn't be so bad, she reasoned. Getting to dress up and spend a night eating and dancing with the English Roses sounded like major awesome fun—just like a dance at school!

As she went downstairs to fix herself a snack, Binah walked through the parlor, as she had done millions of times before. But this time something stopped her. Something about the familiar room was very different.

She paused and looked around. And that's when she saw the pile of large boxes stacked on one side of the room. Taking a closer look, she saw that the boxes were labeled in a familiar, messy script: MISS

FLUFFERNUTTER'S KITCHY KITCHEN SUPPLIES and BOOKS ABOUT BRAIDS.

Suddenly it all made sense! Miss F. had started moving her belongings into the Rossi household. It was logical for Miss Fluffernutter to move into the Rossis' house; she lived by herself in a tiny flat, and the Rossis had a small, but cozy, townhouse with ample room for another person.

Binah looked around to find other unfamiliar objects placed throughout their home. Round lace doilies, of the kind her Nonna and Great-aunt Bea fancied, seemed to cover every available surface. Scented candles were placed haphazardly around the room, along with incense burners, small statues, and other strange items that Binah wasn't used to seeing around her home.

Binah sank into her favorite overstuffed recliner and began to think. A slightly disturbed feeling crept over her. She was happy to have Miss Fluffernutter living with them, but it was peculiar indeed to actually see her teacher's things strewn about the house. She was so used to seeing their parlor a certain way. Everything had been exactly the same for as long as she could remember.

But it wasn't Miss Fluffernutter's sudden presence in the room that bothered her. No, it wasn't the *presence* of Miss Fluffernutter as much as it was the *absence* of her mother. As she thought, Binah realized that what she felt wasn't discomfort as much as guilt. As far as she knew, her dear mum had decorated this room before she had died, and her father had never changed a thing. Binah had always been somewhat comforted by the fact that their parlor was left exactly as her mum had wanted it. And now that Miss Fluffernutter was moving in, things would have to change.

Her face hot with guilt, Binah looked up to the ceiling. Would her mother be upset to see the parlor changed? Would she blame Binah for letting it happen?

CHAPTER 5

Chippie Shop Wednesdays

Wednesdays can mean many things to many people: "hump" day, that glorious "week's half over" feeling, that "Friday's still three days away" pit of dread in the tummy. For some people, it's the day their abs-fave show is on the telly, or the day mashed potatoes are served in the cafeteria, or maybe even the day they wear their favorite pair of socks.

To Binah, however, Wednesdays were so special she had even named them Chippie Shop Wednesdays. (For all you soooo-not-with-it Americans, a "chippie"—often referred to as a chip shop—is sort of a British term for "diner," a greasy place to eat that most traditional of British fast foods: fish and chips.) Every Wednesday since Binah was a little girl, she and her father would eat a lovely dinner of fish and chips at their favorite dining spot, Tiny Tim's. Though Binah usually cooked dinner for the two of them to save money, Mr. Rossi insisted on this small luxury every single week. Binah knew it reminded him of her mother, since the two had gone to Tim's on their first date.

Binah loved Tiny Tim's, with its Plexiglas countertops and bottomless Styrofoam cups of fountain soda, and Tim himself always behind the counter in a faded T-shirt and white apron. Tim wasn't so tiny (fish and chips aren't exactly a healthy, low-fat meal, after all!), but he had a heart as big as his belly, and Binah loved answering his questions about school and hearing stories about his former life as a rock star. (Before opening the chippie, Tim had toured the world as a bona fide rock-and-roll guitarist. He had met all sorts of fabulous actors, actresses, and musicians on his many adventures!)

On this particular Wednesday evening, Binah had arrived home from a lovely day in the park to find a note from her papa waiting on the kitchen table. This is what it said:

DEAR BINAH,

MISS F. AND I ARE OUT AND ABOUT ON A WEDDING CAKE RUN. DON'T WORRY, I HAVEN'T FORGOTTEN OUR CHIPPIE DATE. I WILL MEET YOU AT OUR USUAL SPOT AT 8 PM.

LOVE YOU,

PAPA

P.S. PROMISE TO BRING BACK SOME CAKE SAMPLES FOR YOU!

Binah smiled, carefully folded the note, and put it in her pocket. She was especially excited about Tiny Tim's. The truth is, planning a wedding—

TINY TIM'S
FISH & CHIPS

even a small one—is a lot of work. Papa had been so busy shopping for things like flowers, invitations, and wine with Miss Fluffernutter, Binah felt as if she hadn't seen him in weeks.

Binah glanced at the dingy clock on the wall of Tiny Tim's: 8:30. Where was Papa?

"Still waitin' on your old man, eh?" Tim asked. "I think another soda might make the time pass faster!"

Binah smiled. "Thanks, Tim. I-I'm not sure what happened. He said he'd meet me at 8 PM. It's not like Papa to be late like this."

Tim nodded. "Dude, plannin' a weddin' sure is tricky. I bet he just got held up somewhere."

Binah looked down at her soda and shrugged. "I'm sure that's it." She hoped her voice sounded more convinced than she felt.

"Ah. I remember when your mum and dad came in here on their first date." Tim smiled as he set another Coke in front of Binah.

Binah rested her head on her hands. "Tell me the story again," she pleaded. No matter how many times she had heard Tim tell the tale of her parents' first date at the chippie, Binah still loved hearing it.

Tim grinned, then ruffled Binah's wavy blond hair playfully. "I can't keep tellin' these same stories with your dad marryin' a new gal!"

Binah considered this. "I suppose not," she said. She imagined how awkward Miss Fluffernutter might feel hearing stories about Binah's mother and father being romantic on their first date. She didn't want Miss F. to feel awkward. At the same time, though, Binah would miss hearing Tim's stories about her mum.

"Can you tell it to me one last time?" she pleaded. "For old time's sake?"

"Oh, all right." He folded his arms across his chest and scratched the stubble on his chin. "Now, let's see. It was a long time ago—I can't even remember the year now—when your papa brought your mama here for the first time. Barely had a penny to his name, but he treated her like she was Her Majesty, the queen herself—he just worshipped her. Prettiest thing I've ever seen, too. She was radiant.

"She laughed a lot. I remember that. Your mum had a sweet laugh—magical, sorta, like the tinkling of bells. Never heard anything like it until your papa brought you in here when you were just a wee thing. I swear, you and your mum could be twins." Tim went to answer the ringing phone.

Binah smiled and sipped her Coke. She loved

hearing these stories about her mum, especially about the way her mum used to laugh at her father's silly, corny jokes. She liked to imagine the two of them sitting where she was now, giggling and chatting and having a grand time.

Tim appeared at her table again. "That was your father, Binah," he said with a smile. "He's waiting for you back at home."

Startled, Binah reached for her purse. "Um, okay," she said, confused as to why her father would change plans so suddenly. "How much do I owe you, Tim?"

Tim smiled and put up his hand to stop her. "Soda's on me, love. Now, run along home!"

The front door heaved a sigh as Binah entered her house. She could hear the sound of laughter, and her nose tingled as she inhaled the scent of food. "Hello?" she called out tentatively.

"In here, Binah," her father called from the kitchen. "Miss Fluffernutter is making dinner for us!"

Binah stepped into the kitchen to find her father and Miss Fluffernutter flushed and giggly.

"Papa, where were you?" she asked. "I was worried!"

Mr. Rossi's smile disappeared. "Binah. I'm very sorry. We got carried away trying different cakes, and I didn't realize that it had become so late. By the time we got back here, Miss F. offered to cook us all a nice dinner."

"I'm making a special surprise, Binah," Miss Fluffernutter said with a smile.

"Yes," Mr. Rossi continued, "we both think you'll quite like it. Anyway, Miss F. isn't a fan of fish and chips, and I thought it would be nice if we all ate together, as a family."

Miss Fluffernutter beamed. Binah forced herself to smile, but on the inside, she was rather miffed. Honestly, she had seen her father so rarely lately that she had been looking forward to spending some time with him alone, just the two of them. *Does that make me a horrible person?* she wondered.

Well, I think we both know the answer to that. Binah is anything but a horrible person. The English Roses would be the first to tell you how kind and generous and thoughtful Binah always was—especially when it came to her papa. No, Binah wasn't a bad person at all. She was just having a hard time adjusting to her father having to fit a new woman into his life—even if that woman was someone she adored, like Miss Fluffernutter. Anyway, that is neither here nor there. Back to the story, yo!

As they all sat down at the table, Miss Fluffernutter was

babbling away about all of the glorious wedding cakes they had sampled. "Can you believe," she chattered, "that they have cakes with actual flowers that you can eat now? And they're real? I mean, what will they come up with next?" As she spoke, she removed a piping hot creation from the oven and placed it on the kitchen table.

"This looks mouthwatering!" Binah's father whistled in appreciation.

"What is it?" Binah asked curiously. It didn't look like any dish she had seen before, but smelled delicious.

"It's shepherd's pie," Miss Fluffernutter responded cheerfully. "Foo-Foo Fluffernutter's family recipe!"

Binah stifled a giggle, but made it sound as if she

was coughing to be polite. Rudeness was not her thing, but come on! What kind of a silly name was that? "Foo-Foo Fluffernutter?" she sputtered.

"Yes, my dear mummy," Miss F. replied. "She lives in Coventry, but she'll be down for the wedding. You'll love her!"

Mr. Rossi shoved a mouthful of the hot pie into his mouth, then closed his eyes in delight. "This," he murmured, "is heavenly. It even rivals your mother's, Binah!"

Binah tried the shepherd's pie. She had to admit that it tasted quite yummy, even though it was nothing like her mum's.

At this, Binah felt a sharp pang in her chest. It wasn't the pain of hunger, or the pain her lungs felt when she ran too much in gym class. It was a pain that's as old as the tradition of British high tea: the pain of guilt. Binah felt guilty that she and her papa were enjoying Miss Fluffernutter's shepard's pie as much as they had enjoyed Binah's mum's.

Binah volunteered to do the dishes that night. Her father and Miss Fluffernutter had guest list business to take care of, and quite honestly, Binah simply felt like being alone with a pile of dirty dishes and warm, soapy water. Sometimes the most mindless tasks are endlessly comforting.

CHAPTER 6

Spilling the Beans

Two weeks later, Binah invited the English Roses over to help clean her house. Now, hold up, I know what you're thinking: *Wow* (sarcastic roll of the eyes), *that sure sounds like fun.* Well, you see, my dears, the English Roses are such true-blue besties that they will willingly sacrifice a lovely summer afternoon in order to help a sista out.

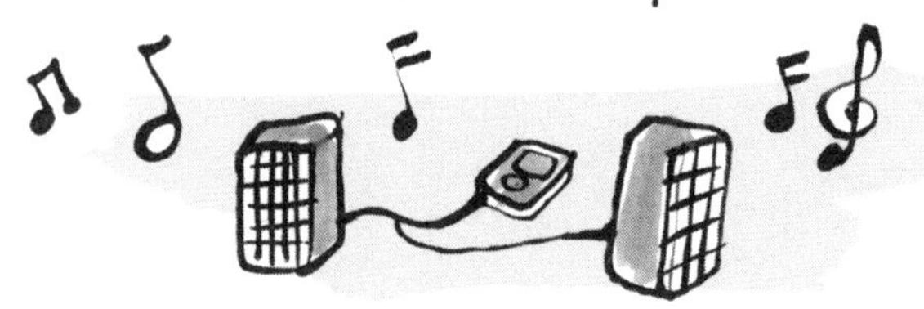

And help was sorely needed! With Miss Fluffernutter still in the process of moving, Binah had realized that the Rossis needed to clear out some space in their house for all of her stuff. That meant cleaning out the attic. Ugh. Shivers. I'm sure some of you readers have an attic at home that gives you the willies as well. I suppose attics are just intrinsically (a word that Nicole would tell you means "naturally") creepy places, filled with spiders and cold drafts and dusty boxes of old junk with mice hiding inside. *Eek!*

The Roses were, of course, making the most of the task at hand. Charlotte had brought her iPod and speakers, and the

Dancing their cares away

funky sounds of the girls' favorite artist, Lizzie Love, were blaring. Amy couldn't help but swivel her hips to the beat as she sifted through the contents of a cardboard box.

"Lizzie Love is just the end all." She sighed, shaking her head of red curls in time to the music.

"Totes," Nicole agreed.

"The mostest," Grace added.

"TDF," Charlotte chimed in. (TDF is an abbreviation for To Die For, in case you didn't know!) She held up a teeny, tiny pink onesie. "Aww, was this yours, Binah?" She giggled.

Binah smiled, then blushed. "Yeah," she said, "I suppose it was at one point."

Grace let out a holler. "I've hit pay dirt!"

she cried. She held up a dusty album with the word PHOTOGRAPHS etched on it in fine gold letters.

The Roses all ooh'ed and ahh'ed over the pictures inside. There were photos of Binah's mum and dad when they were young, smiling, holding hands, kissing under an umbrella in the rain. There were many pictures of Binah's mum when she was pregnant, too.

"Gosh, Binah," Amy observed. "Your mum was such a hottie."

"Yeah," Nicole added. "And you two look exactly alike. You could be twins!"

Binah glanced hopefully at her friends. "Really?" she asked. The Roses nodded solemnly.

Binah took the photo album from Amy's hands and slowly began turning the pages. Without realizing it, her eyes welled up with tears.

The rest of the Roses glanced at one another in concern.

"Binah," Nicole said, staring straight into the eyes of her flaxen-haired friend, "I know it must be really hard to go through all this old stuff of your

mum's. All of these reminders. Is everything okay?"

"Binah, come on," Grace said gently. "Talk to us."

Binah took a deep breath. "Well," she began, "I love Miss Fluffernutter. I'm really excited for her to marry Papa."

Charlotte interrupted, nodding in understanding. "We know you are, Binah," she said.

"But," Binah continued, "at the same time, I have been feeling rather . . . guilty."

Grace frowned. "Why do you feel guilty, Bee?"

Binah wasn't sure how to describe her feelings. "I guess—maybe this sounds silly, but I feel like I am somehow betraying my mum."

"Oooh." The rest of the Roses nodded in sympathy.

"I know I never had the chance to get to know her. But she's always felt so real to me. I feel her watching over me every single day." At this, even more tears filled Binah's eyes. "And just the thought of changing the house—you know, redecorating and moving stuff around—it's almost like . . . I want things to stay the way they were when she was still alive. I imagine her looking down on me from above and feeling sad, or hurt, that Papa and I are moving on."

The Roses enclosed Binah in a five-person hug—no easy feat, let me assure you, but one which they had become pretty good at through the years.

"I understand, Bee," Amy said soothingly, rubbing her friend's back.

Grace nodded. "I think it's totally normal," she said. "But you have nothing to feel guilty about."

Charlotte piped up. "You're the sweetest person in the world, Binah," she added. "It must be hard to have someone else in your dad's life after it's been only the two of you for so long."

Binah removed an embroidered handkerchief from her pocket and dabbed at her eyes. (Yes, a

handkerchief! Perhaps it sounds old-fashioned, but Binah is just an old-fashioned kind of girl!)

"Hey, I have an idea," Amy offered. "Why don't we take a break from cleaning and practice our dance moves? We're going to need to brush up before the wedding reception!"

"That's a great idea!" Charlotte responded. Nicole and Grace nodded their heads in agreement. Each could clearly see what Amy was thinking. Dancing was sure to put a smile on Binah's face.

In case you didn't know, the English Roses are faboo dancers! They even won first place in their school's talent competition last year. They are known throughout their school not only for their fresh moves, but for inventing new steps that seem

to always become the latest craze. They danced their old favorite standbys—the Hullabaloo, the Techno Fox-Trot, the Watusi—and also brought out a few recent faves, like the Higgle-Bump, the Ninney-Finney, and the Ground Round. As they danced and swayed to the music, they became a blur of leaping legs and flailing arms, sweaty and flushed. Binah could feel the stresses of the past weeks melting away as she furiously danced.

Suddenly, a low growling sound could be heard above the soulful voice of Lizzie Love. The girls looked at one another in alarm.

Again the sound reverberated through the room. This time, it seemed to be louder.

"BRRRRRAAAAAPPP."

Amy turned down the speakers.

"Binah, did you get a dog?" Charlotte asked nervously.

"A big, scary dog?" Nicole shuddered.

Grace pointed sheepishly to her tummy. "Um, no. That's my stomach," she said. "I'm starrrrvving."

The other Roses giggled. Soon the giggles turned into chuckles, which turned into loud guffaws. They grasped their bellies, and Amy even rolled on the floor, howling. Nicole's face was beet

red, and tears ran down her cheeks. Charlotte laughed so hard she snorted, which just caused the others to laugh even harder.

"Yep," Nicole said once they'd recovered. "Sounds like our Grace."

"Well, you're in luck," Binah told her. "I made a big batch of rhubarb scones this morning, and I'll brew a fresh pot of tea to go with!"

The girls moved to the kitchen, and as they munched, they ooh'ed and ahh'ed over Binah's scones.

That evening before they left, the English Roses gave Binah plenty of hugs and support. Life might not always be easy, but having the four best friends in the entire world sure helps you get through the rough patches!

CHAPTER 7

The Notebook

The next day each of the English Roses received a phone call from Binah.

"Meet at Charlotte's tonight. Seven PM," she said breathlessly, then hung up. The Roses were puzzled. It wasn't like Binah to be so brief, even curt, on the phone. They knew something big must have happened.

MOUI

That night at 7 PM sharp the Roses gathered in Charlotte's bedroom. Since Charlotte lived in a bona fide mansion, her house was the go-to destination for the Roses' MOUI (that's Meetings of Utmost Importance, of course). As usual, Charlotte was prepared with snacks from Nigella, the family cook. She passed out pigs in blankets and peanut butter pretzels. Everyone munched in silence, except for Binah, who refused the food.

She looked at her friends gravely. "So, listen to this," she began. "Last night I was up in the attic, going through things one final time to see if there was anything we missed during

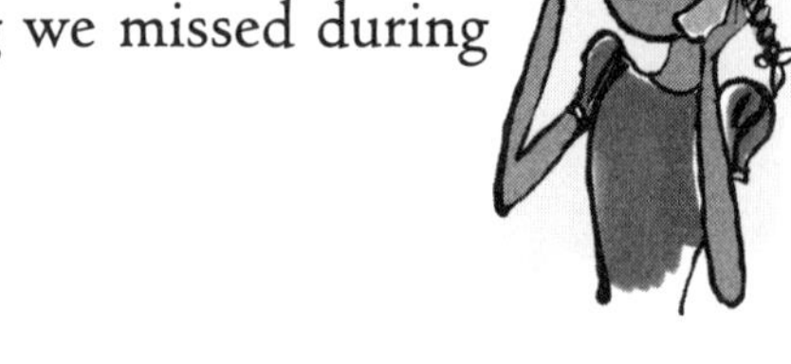

the day. I found a box shoved deep into a corner. I guess no one had seen it. So I opened it and started going through its contents. And I found this."

From her backpack Binah produced a small notebook with a worn leather cover. "It belonged to my mum," she whispered.

All of the girls stopped eating.

Amy put her hand to her mouth. "Oh my—"

"No way!" A pretzel fell out of Grace's mouth.

Binah's fingers trembled as she opened the journal. "Yes," she said. "It was hers. I stayed up all night reading the entire thing in my bed with a flashlight. I don't know why, but I didn't want Papa to know that I'd found it."

The other Roses nodded understandingly.

"What did it say, Binah?" Nicole asked, curious.

"Well," Binah began, "it said a lot of things, actually. Things about my dad. Things about . . . me, too." Binah took a deep breath. "I think my mum wrote part of it after she got really sick."

Charlotte reached out and put her arms around Binah.

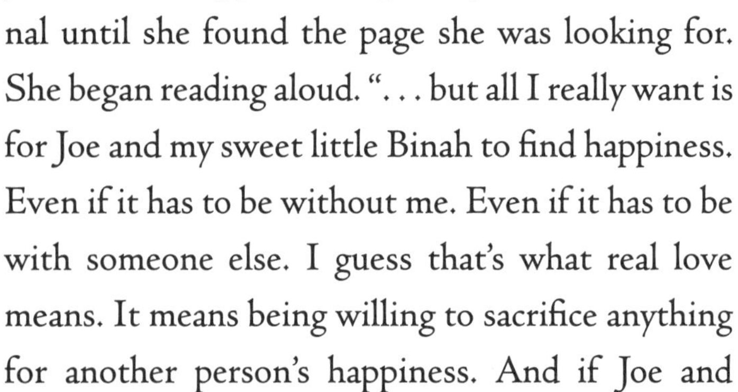

"Do you want to talk about it?" Grace asked gently.

"Actually, it made me feel better to read it," Binah said. "Especially this part." Binah flipped through the journal until she found the page she was looking for. She began reading aloud. ". . . but all I really want is for Joe and my sweet little Binah to find happiness. Even if it has to be without me. Even if it has to be with someone else. I guess that's what real love means. It means being willing to sacrifice anything for another person's happiness. And if Joe and

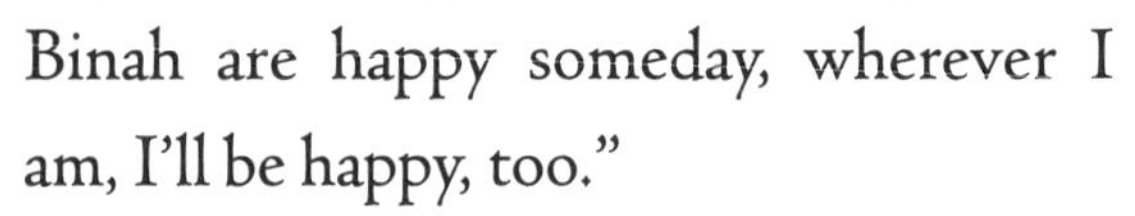

Binah are happy someday, wherever I am, I'll be happy, too."

Binah stopped reading. The other Roses were sniffling. Grace blew her

nose loudly into a tissue. For a long time, no one spoke.

Finally, Amy broke the silence. "Wow," she said. "That's so . . ."

"Powerful," Nicole finished for her. She dabbed her eyes. "It's beautiful, Binah."

"I know," Binah said softly. "And it means that . . . I don't have to feel guilty anymore. I know my mum just wants Papa and me to be happy. And we are happy with Miss Fluffernutter."

"And we are so happy for all of you!" Charlotte cried, giving Binah a big hug. The other Roses followed suit. Five-way hugs were their specialty.

"Thanks, guys," Binah said. "I don't know what I'd do

without you! I really appreciate you all getting together at such short notice. I just had to share this with you face-to-face."

"Um, sorry, Binah, but when has getting together at Charlotte's and stuffing our faces ever been a problem?" Grace said. The other girls had to laugh.

"Oh!" Binah said, clapping her hand over her mouth. "I almost forgot to tell you guys. So, after I read through the journal, I had to wake up my papa and tell him all about it. It just didn't feel right not to share it with him. And you know what he told me? He said that he actually redecorated the entire house after Mum died, because it was too painful to leave it as it was."

"So it's not like you're undoing your mum's decorating," Nicole finished Binah's thought.

"Exactly," she said. "I feel so much better. I feel like this huge weight has been lifted from my shoulders."

The other Roses could tell. For the first time in weeks, Binah's face looked clear and worry free.

CHAPTER 8

Give Me a Moment, Please

The days passed by like lightning zigzagging through the sky. You know how summer tends to do that? You wake up one day, and it's almost time to go (ugh, those three dreaded words!) back to school.

Well, time seems to pass even more quickly with wedding planning in full throttle. There was so much to do, in fact, that Binah hardly realized the days were going by. And soon it was the day of the wedding.

Binah's house was like a zoo! Though her own family was small as can be, Miss Fluffernutter had oodles of relatives in town for the event. Binah could hardly keep all of their names straight. Auntie Mamie, Cousin Hamish, little Ginger—the names and faces all seemed to run into one another in a total blur! Binah wasn't used to seeing so many people in the hallways of her tiny house, or

so many bodies cluttering the kitchen where she spent so much time alone cooking for her papa.

Binah had escaped to her room, away from the crowds of people. Sitting in her lovely new dress, with her makeup done to a T (Amy had come over earlier and applied it with

a perfect flair) and her hair in a sweeping updo, she was trying to clear her head a bit before the limo came to take her, Miss F., and the rest of the wedding party to Charlotte's house for the big ceremony. (Binah was totally excited to ride in a real limousine! Of course, she had been driven in Charlotte's family's Rolls Royce plenty of times, but that's not exactly the same thing.)

There was a gentle knock on the door. "Come in," Binah said in her usual soft tone.

the Most Beautiful Bride in the World

The door creaked open, and Miss Fluffernutter stood before her. Only she didn't look like the frizzy-haired, frazzled teacher Binah knew so well. Instead, Binah was staring at the most beautiful bride she had ever seen. Miss Fluffernutter's usually frizzy hair hung in soft ringlets that framed her face so that she resembled an angel. On her head was a small wreath of flowers. Ivory satin crinkles with tiny beads of flowers made up the bodice of her dress, which hung in a simple, straight sheath down to her feet. Her cheeks glowed with a rosy happiness that seemed to radiate from within.

"You look beautiful." Binah breathed softly.

"Thank you, Binah." Miss Fluffernutter smiled. "Though I do feel funny not wearing anything with color! You look radiant yourself." She paused.

"Do you have a minute?"

"Of course," she said.

Miss Fluffernutter went to take a seat on Binah's bed, then clamped her hand over her mouth. "Oh my!" she said. "I'd better not sit down or I'll wrinkle the dickens out of this dress! I suppose I'll just stand here. Though I do feel silly just standing while you're sitting."

Binah smiled. She suddenly felt slightly shy and almost awkward, which was not a feeling she was used to around Miss Fluffernutter.

Miss Fluffernutter took her hand. "Binah," she began, "I realize that it might be a little difficult to have your father get remarried. It must be rather strange for you to suddenly have a new woman around all the time."

Binah looked down. She didn't know what to say or how to fight back the tears that were filling her

eyes. It was so hard to lie to Miss Fluffernutter! "Well, I suppose it's been a little hard at times," she admitted, sniffling.

"Of course, my dear." Miss Fluffernutter nodded, then produced a handkerchief and dabbed at Binah's eyes, gently wiping away her tears. "That's to be expected. But I want you to know that I'm not here to come between you and your father. In fact, it is my greatest hope that your relationship

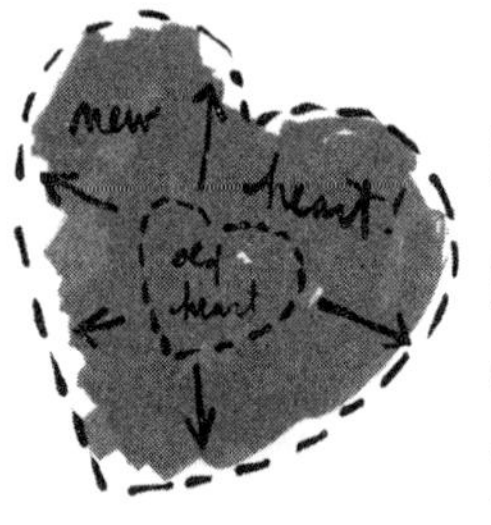

becomes stronger than ever." She paused, then took a breath. "And I don't want to replace your mother. I know that no one ever could."

Miss Fluffernutter smiled and continued. "Sometimes I think . . . now, maybe this sounds silly, but I truly believe that when your family expands, it only makes your heart bigger, too, because there is that much more love inside. Though it may be a difficult adjustment at first, in the end the more people we love, the richer our lives. I promise."

Binah really couldn't believe how much she was crying! She was sure her eye makeup would now qualify as a full-fledged, raccoonlike fashion "don't," but she didn't care. Well, can you blame her? Quite an emotional moment, if I do say so myself. I mean, I'm even sniffling over here. Give me a moment, please.

"I know you're right, Miss Fluffernutter," Binah said, wiping her eyes and smiling.

"You are the most important person in your father's life," Miss Fluffernutter assured her. "He loves no one more than you. And nothing is going to change that."

Right then, Binah knew exactly what Miss Fluffernutter meant. Because it was as if she could feel her heart growing. She realized that having one more person in her family—especially someone as special as Miss F.—could only increase the love and happiness in her life.

"Well," Miss Fluffernutter said, offering her

hand to Binah. “As the Americans say, I think it’s time to get this show on the road!”

But the show wasn’t road-ready, it seems, for at that instant, the door whipped open and in flew Charlotte, breathless and red faced.

“Miss Fluffernutter!” she gasped, almost in tears. “We have a BIG problem! I think—I think we’re going to have to call off the wedding!”

Here comes the bride.

CHAPTER 9

Uh-oh

Miss Fluffernutter had Charlotte sit down on Binah's bed, take a few deep breaths, and calm down as best she could. "Now, Charlotte, please tell me what exactly is going on," she urged.

Poor Charlotte tried to compose herself, but she was clearly frazzled beyond belief. "I don't know where I should even begin, Miss F.!" she wailed. "First, the flower girl wet her pants . . . or should I say, her dress! Then the florist arrived with the wrong flowers. These were supposed to go to a funeral on the other side of town, but there was a mix-up and there's no time to send them back! And if that wasn't enough, Hillary is apparently allergic to these new flowers. Her face swelled up like a tomato, and she had to leave to go to the DOCTOR!" Hillary was the other bridesmaid.

Poor Charlotte. Well, wouldn't you be upset, too? That is quite a lot of disasters for one small, humble little wedding. And she had worked very hard to help plan the whole thing.

Binah looked at Miss Fluffernutter, unsure if the teacher would cry or yell or burst out in an hysterical fit of rage. She had seen enough episodes of the reality television show *Monster Bride* at Charlotte's house to know how a bride could act when the teeniest, tiniest thing went wrong on her wedding day. Binah fully expected Miss F. to burst into tears, or turn a strange shade of purple, or perhaps explode. Instead . . .

Miss Fluffernutter started giggling. The giggles turned into chuckles. The chuckles turned into big-bellied laughs, which turned into huge guffaws. She threw back her head and laughed and laughed and laughed some more.

Binah and Charlotte looked at each other, alarmed. This wasn't exactly the reaction either was expecting. But it was too hard to resist Miss F.'s infectious laughter. Both girls started twittering themselves, and soon they were laughing so hard they were holding their bellies.

Once they had calmed themselves, Miss Fluffernutter sighed. "Oh dear. I think we all

needed that! I mean, it is quite unfortunate about Hillary. I do hope she's all right! And poor little Astrid, I bet she feels just awful. As for the flowers, oh well. What can one do when life hands you these small disasters? The important thing is that the people I love are here to see me marry the man I love."

This made Binah smile. She truly felt so lucky to have Miss Fluffernutter in her life!

"But Miss F.," Charlotte protested, "the only bridesmaid you have left is Binah. She can't walk down the aisle alone! It's bad luck!"

Binah wrinkled her nose. "It is? I've never heard that."

Charlotte looked unsure. "Well—well, I mean, it can't be *good* luck!"

Miss Fluffernutter shrugged. "I know it isn't what we planned, dear, but I think it's what's going to have to happen. I can't see another way out of it."

Just then Binah stood up, a lightning bolt flashing inside her head. "Wait a minute," she said, a smile playing on her lips. "I know where we can get some last-minute bridesmaids."

CHAPTER 10

Who's That Coming Down the Aisle?

Charlotte's backyard had been transformed into a page out of a fairy-tale storybook. Garlands of flowers hung about a hand-carved wooden gazebo, which was wreathed in dozens of tiny, twinkling lights. An aisle of

white, also lined with brilliant lights, led up to the gazebo. Birds chirped and bees hummed in the perfectly landscaped flowers, bushes, and trees that were strategically placed throughout the yard. A string quartet provided a gentle accompaniment to the sounds of nature.

The wedding guests, seated on either side of the aisle, were glancing at their watches with

impatience. It was already fifteen minutes past three o'clock. The wedding was supposed to have started at three. Murmurs could be heard rippling through the small crowd, and ladies started fanning themselves with the wedding programs in impatience. What was the holdup? What was going on?

Mr. Rossi, standing near the front of the gazebo, shifted his weight and glanced around nervously.

You can just imagine what was going through his head as he saw the bewildered looks of his guests! What if Miss Fluffernutter had decided that she didn't want to marry him? What if she had a case of what is commonly referred to as "cold feet"?

Just then a woman with a gray bun, warm, crinkly eyes, and a big smile walked to the front of the gazebo. She politely cleared her throat. "May I have your attention, everyone?" She spoke clearly, her voice lilting through the summer air. "For those of you who don't know me, I am Foo-Foo Fluffernutter, Miss Fluffernutter's mother. I just wanted to let you know that there were a few . . . complications . . . with the wedding party, but everything has been taken care of

and the ceremony shall commence now. Thank you for your patience!"

The string quartet started playing a lovely tune, and all heads turned to watch the procession. But who appeared walking down the aisle? Not one, not three, but all five English Roses, each holding a small bouquet and wearing a huge smile.

You see, all along Binah had hoped that her four best friends could somehow be a part of the wedding ceremony, and when Miss F.'s other bridesmaid had fallen ill, it seemed the perfect opportunity for the Roses to get their own walk down the aisle! Each wore her best dress. Miss Fluffernutter didn't care that they all didn't match; she was just happy to have five of her favorite students as part of her big day.

The ceremony was beautiful. Even Grace could be heard sniffling from her place in the front row. Next to her, Amy blew her nose loudly, which caused Nicole to giggle.

Charlotte nudged her sharply. "Quit it!" she hissed, not wanting anything to disturb the ceremony.

Finally, the minister pronounced the couple "husband and wife," and Charlotte couldn't help but let out a squeal as Mr. Rossi lifted Miss Fluffernutter's veil to kiss her. The string quartet started up a joyful song as the couple walked back down the aisle hand in hand. Before they did so, though, both Mr. Rossi and Miss Fluffernutter kissed Binah and hugged her as tightly as they could.

Binah sighed, tears shining in her eyes. *So this,* she thought, *is what perfect happiness feels like!*

CHAPTER II

Flying Flowers

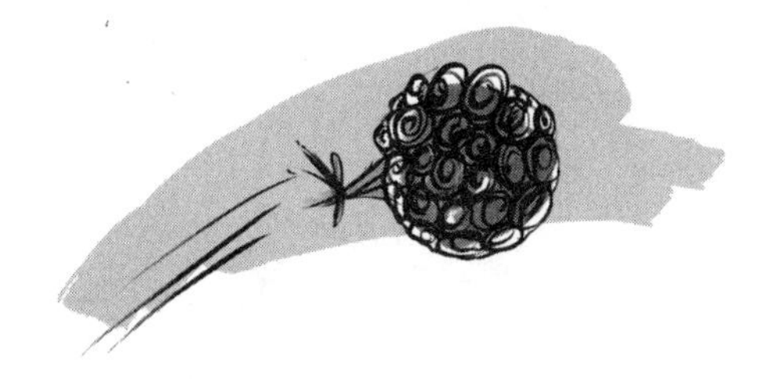

You surely don't think our story ends there, do you? I'd hope not! For as everyone knows, the best part of any wedding isn't the ceremony but the reception. And this particular wedding reception was more bangin' than any seen on either side of the pond.

Taking advantage of the Ginsbergs' totally gorg backyard and garden area, huge tents had been pitched to accommodate the wedding guests. Beautiful candle centerpieces adorned each table. Each candle emitted a soft glow that perfectly highlighted the heaping bunches of fresh cut flowers and tiny white lights decorating the tent.

And the food! Nigella had been recruited to make all of her specialties. There was roast beef, fresh fish, bangers and mash, and of course, by

special request, shepherd's pie (Binah gave Nigella her recipe)! Everyone ate and ate and ate until their bellies couldn't take anymore—especially the English Roses!

In the midst of eating, one guest started rapping on his wine glass with a knife, producing a loud, clanking sound. Others followed suit, until the room was filled with a symphony of clanking. Binah covered her ears. What on earth were these people doing? She couldn't imagine why they were making such a racket!

Charlotte, seeing Binah's look of confusion, leaned over and whispered, "They're trying to get your papa and Miss F. to kiss!"

Sure enough, soon Miss F. leaned over and planted one squarely on Mr. Rossi's lips. The clanging stopped and was replaced by a round of joyous clapping. Binah couldn't help but smile.

Once all the guests had stuffed themselves silly, it was Mr. Rossi's turn to rap on his wine glass with a knife. "Can I have everyone's attention?" he asked, standing.

The guests stopped talking and put down their silverware. Mr. Rossi took a deep breath and began speaking.

"I just wanted to take a moment and thank you all for being here today," he said. Turning to Miss F., who gave him a bright smile, he continued. "I feel like the luckiest man in the world to have found such a wonderful woman who loves me exactly for who I am. Real love is something rare

and precious, and I think everyone should treat it as such."

He went on. "Moreover, I want to thank my daughter, Binah, who led me to my new bride. Without her, we probably would have never met. Binah, I love you more than anything in the world, and I can't wait for our new life as a family to start together." With that, Binah rose, tears in her eyes, and hugged and kissed her father.

Well, after that emotional speech, there was nary a dry eye in the crowd. To lighten the mood, Grace

grabbed the microphone. "And now, people, I think it's time for everyone to get their dance ON!"

Appreciative applause from the audience sounded as the DJ (a nerdy but sweet boy in the Roses' class

at school who called himself MC Drip Drop due to his problematic postnasal drip) took the stage. There was hardly any spare room on the dance floor as everyone moved to the beat. Luckily, Miss Fluffernutter had plenty of cute nephews for the English Roses to dance with. And, wouldn't you know, even Foo-Foo Fluffernutter took to the floor, showing the English Roses some of the slick dance moves from her own day.

"She's not bad," Grace whispered to Binah as a crowd gathered around to cheer on the older woman.

Sweaty and happy, dancing with new friends and old, Binah couldn't remember when she last felt so good. Until . . .

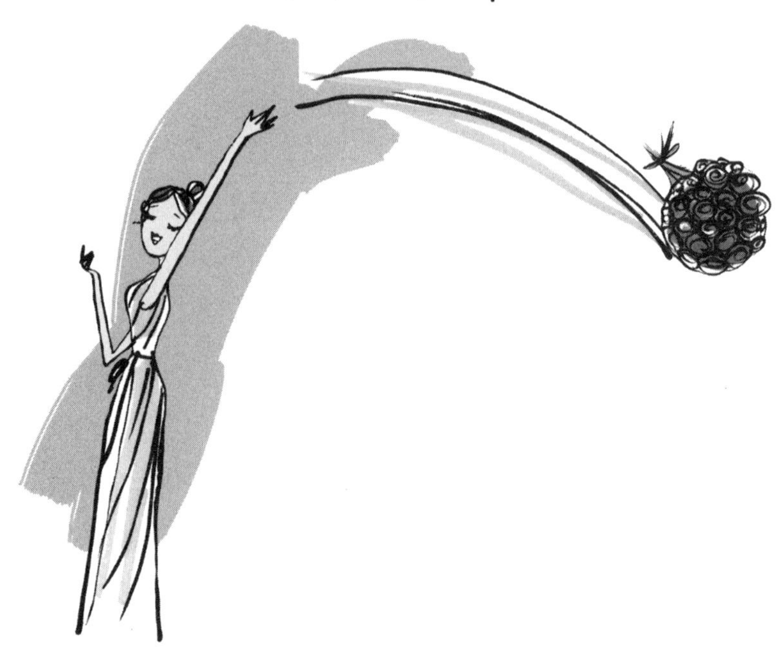

TWEEET. A loud, piercing whistle halted the music. "Listen up, ladies," Grace called. "It's time for Miss F. to throw her bouquet!"

A murmur rippled through the crowd as all the single ladies gathered behind Miss Fluffernutter. *Hmmm,* Binah thought. *Another wedding tradition I don't understand.* But she stood patiently beside Nicole as everyone jostled for the best spot.

With her back to the crowd, Miss Fluffernutter threw her bouquet in the air. The flowers sailed in a high arc.

"Nice throw, Miss F.!" Grace couldn't help but shout.

Women were darting left and right, trying to get closer to the flying floral arrangement. Not one to push and shove, Binah stood patiently near the back of the crowd. She closed her eyes. She reached her hands up high.

And the bouquet flew right into her waiting arms.

Startled, Binah's eyelids flew open. The wedding guests applauded as the other Roses gathered around their blond friend. "All right, Binah!" Amy shrieked, hugging her friend and jumping up and down excitedly. "You caught the bouquet!"

"What does that mean?" Binah asked, puzzled.

Miss Fluffernutter came over and gave Binah a tight squeeze. "Why, my dear, it means that you'll be the next to get married!" She laughed.

Binah looked from Miss F.'s laughing eyes to her father's silly grin. "That's fine by me," she confessed, giggling. "Because I'm starting to really like weddings!"

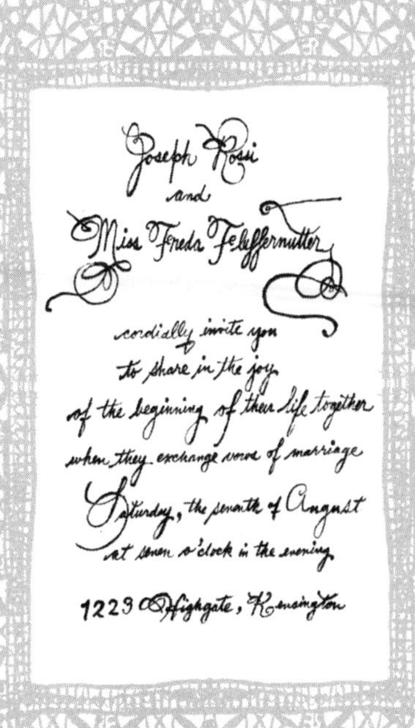

The End

Previous Books by Madonna

PICTURE BOOKS:

The English Roses
Mr. Peabody's Apples
Yakov and the Seven Thieves
The Adventures of Abdi
Lotsa de Casha
The English Roses: Too Good To Be True

CHAPTER BOOKS:

Friends For Life!
Good-Bye, Grace?
The New Girl
A Rose by Any Other Name
Big-Sister Blues
Being Binah
Hooray for the Holidays!
A Perfect Pair
Runway Rose
Ready, Set, Vote!
American Dreams

MADONNA was born in Bay City, Michigan, and now lives in New York with her children, Lola, Rocco, David, and Mercy. She has recorded 18 albums and appeared in 18 movies. This is the twelfth in her series of chapter books. She has also written six picture books for children, starting with the international bestseller *The English Roses,* which was released in 40 languages and more than 100 countries.

JEFFREY FULVIMARI was born in Akron, Ohio. He started coloring when he was two, and has never stopped. Soon after graduating from The Cooper Union in New York City, he began drawing for magazines and television commercials around the globe. He currently lives in a log cabin in upstate New York, and is happiest when surrounded by stacks of paper and magic markers.

A NOTE ON THE TYPE:

This book is set in Mazarin, a "humanist" typeface designed by Jonathan Hoefler. Mazarin is a revival of the typeface of Nicolas Jenson, the fifteenth-century typefounder who created one of the first roman printing types.

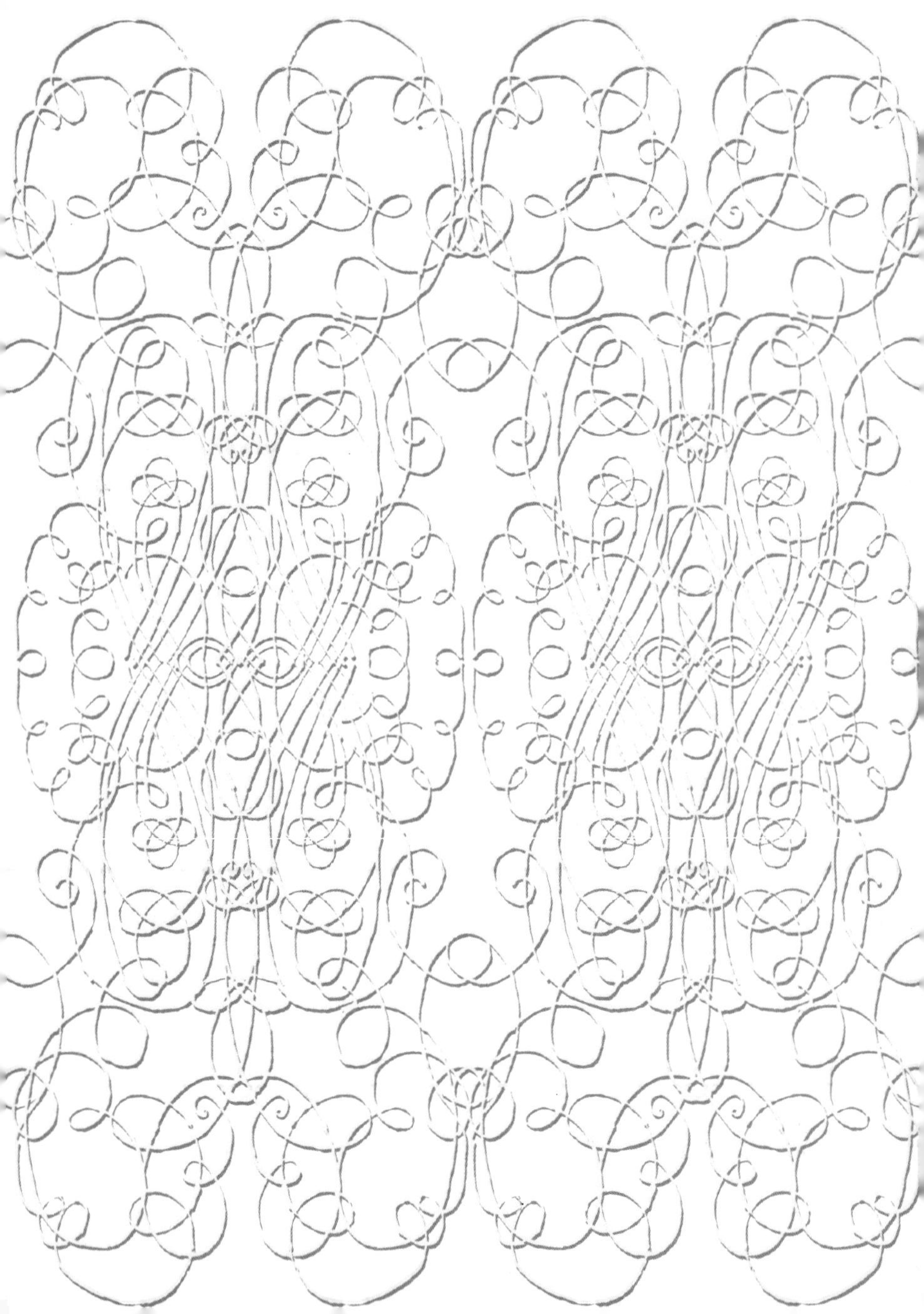